TINY PRIDE
&
PLENTY PREJUDICE

F.T. Barbini and A. Burns

First Published 2015 by Luna Press Publishing

Text Copyright © F.T. Barbini & A. Burns 2009
Cover design by © F.T. Barbini 2015
Portrait by Merry-Joseph Blondel

All rights reserved. No part of this publication may be reproduced, stored in a retrieval system, or transmitted, in any form or by any means without the prior written permission of the copyright owners. Nor can it be circulated in any form of binding or cover other than that in which it is published and without similar condition including this condition being imposed on a subsequent purchaser.

All characters in this publication are fictitious and any resemblance to real persons, living or dead is purely coincidental.

*For those who like to read
Jane Austen's entire body of work,
while squashed into tiny cars,
as they travel from Edinburgh to Rome and
back.*

Pumpington Park

My Dearest Heather,

How much time has passed since our first meeting last summer, and how I do miss the society with which we were so lucky to be acquainted with. Pumpington Park is ever so dull at this time of the year, and even more so since the departing of dear mama.

Papa is in low spirits and has been out of society for some time now. It grieves me to think of him here alone, yet my heart wills me to leave this summer. My spirits are not as high as you can imagine and many a night I sit at the pianoforte and play for papa. It is wretched that he relies on my presence, yet how at this time could I possibly refuse it.

How I miss the intercourse with a certain gentleman. You of course, my dearest, will understand me on this point and I shall say no more. Society here is rare and lacks the vibrancy that summer brings it.

I wait in anticipation of your letters, so full of news they always are.

Your devoted friend etc.
Isabella Pumpington

Reumaton Park

My Dearest Isabella,

I sincerely hope that your spirit is somewhat higher since your last letter. The departure of the late Mrs Pumpington has been a shock for us all, though we did expect the passing to occur earlier than it did. Your dearest mother had a strong constitution, and because of that she survived the fall from the White Cliffs of Dover, and carried on living for a few months more. Your devotion to feed the invalid has been greatly talked about here at Reumaton and Lady Felicity Ferocity, who was visiting us just last week, said that she will let the whole society of Bath know of your good heart.

Now, I expect this will be great news for you, since the certain gentleman on whom your thoughts are set has just arrived in Bath. I have received secure knowledge from Mrs Sluttlike that Mr Pea has gone to Bath and will spend the greatest part of his summer there. Therefore I entreat you Isabella, to find a way of bringing your graces to Bath as soon as convenient. If you are able to plan such a journey, then write to me hastily. On my part I would very much like to enjoy the summer society of Bath with you.

Our uncle Phil Wuss will be travelling to Prudence next week and will be passing Pumpington Park to call on you and your father, to express his deepest sympathy for the departure of Mrs Pumpington. Naturally before reaching you he will have passed through Bath, and I believe he will be able to provide you with some knowledge of Mr Sean Pea; Nay! I am sure, since you will be able to obtain whatever information from him that you wish, you skilled friend!

Reumaton is quiet now; most of our friends have made their arrangements to go to their summer dwellings. I am left with the charge of dear Nancy. You will recall she is the 15 year old daughter of my brother, Mr Athol Mouthful and his wife Mrs Lotta Mouthful. She is growing into a well bred, sort of pretty lady, although she will never have my talents, as I am kindly devoted to remind her every day, normally after tea.

Two more pieces of information before I leave you; the family tomb in which my dearest parents rest is finally complete; I know you were expecting this event with trepidation. I can now remove their bodies from the cellar and give them a proper burial.

The second news concerns Mrs Smelly; she asked my leave to host in Reumaton an acquaintance of hers, with her husband, for one night, two days henceforth. So I shall let you know. Write soon my particular friend, so that your letter may fix my oblique posture.

Devotedly yours,
Heather Mouthful

Pumpington Park

Dearest Heather,

I received your letter this morning and must say that I am in the highest of spirits at the thought of us meeting once more. I must of course wait until my dear papa is settled once more, and have already a plan, but must act with utmost discretion until all is resolved. If everything goes well I will be in Bath to experience all of the summer society, and to be with you, my dearest of companions. Oh what lovemaking we shall both accomplish with the young gentlemen of Bath!

Of course I do still think of my dear Peawee, but your mention of Mrs Sluttlike's knowing of him being in Bath has created nervousness in my disposition. As you must know, her eldest daughter, Fanny, recently returned from three months in London where I have heard rumours of her associating with Peawee. Although I am sure of his feelings with regard to myself, I know her to be a devious creature, and until I can be assured of intentions towards me after such a long time apart, I must restrain from making a folly of our relationship.

I look forward to seeing Sir Phil Wuss, our dear uncle, and hope to extract some juicy facts about Mr Pea. I do so hope that he has not been making love to Fanny Sluttlike, or I shall be very vexed.

I am glad to hear of your being in charge of Nancy; she is, as you said, a well-bred young lady, however beauty I cannot bestow on her when thinking of you. Yours is a far superior blood, and comparing her to you is like comparing a donkey to a well bred Stallion. Your attentions I am sure will have a positive effect on her future in society.

The news of your family tomb finally being restored to its rightful place, I must say rests my heart. To think that every day you may visit them in your own ground is the mark of great devotion to one's parents; I can only hope to live up to your standards.

I will write again as soon as my plans for departure to Bath are secured.

Your loyal and devoted companion,
I Pumpington

Reumaton Park

My Erect Cousin Isabella,

It is with immense trepidation that I lay this pen to paper, for what has occurred yestereve has made my heart tremble so much that I thought I was going to join my beloved parents in one instant! Mr Smelly has arrived, and he has brought with him the handsomest of guest!

Yesterday morning I was taking my usual turn in the shrubbery, when I heard steps approaching from the cherry tree. Quickly I seated myself on the beautiful marble bench, and assumed a most pleasing posture, so as not to seem a commoner. Not long was I thusly, that Mr Smelly appeared from the left path, followed by someone that I can only describe as a dream. I stood and greeted the dear Mr Smelly with charm, and was then introduced to his friend.

"My niece," he said, "This is my dear friend, Mr Aragorn Pantsful." I had to struggle to maintain my lady posture and not to faint but, of course, I succeeded. He kissed my hand, and believe me when I say that I thereafter put that glove locked away into a chest!

Mr Pantsful is an admiral of the British fleet, and has been travelling the world since he was six-and-ten. He made his own fortune and name, and the sea has given him that camel appearance, with those eyes that gaze far, so far that in order to look into them, you have at times to jump up and down before him. But I quickly found a way around this: I made Nancy sew under my dress a most comfortable cube of wood, so that when I stop, I can step upon it and look at Mr Pantsful in the eyes. The only drawback is that when I walk I make odd sounds, but we are not vexed about it.

He has truly pleasing manners and is used to delightful society; on no account would I wish to change him. He has been most attentive to me for the entire evening and the following morning, and so pleased was he of this unexpected acquaintance with yours truly, that he requested my leave to stop by on his way back from the North.

I declare that I felt wretched at his departure, and I will not deny to you that I wish his journey full of disgrace and unexpected death of horses, so that he may return earlier.

If he should decide to remain a few weeks in Reumaton, I will have to postpone our meeting in

Bath, for which I should be truly sorry, but when I think of his breed, I cannot check my posture. Your presence here, if that was the case, will be most appreciated, but I suspect that I could convince him to join us in Bath, because no man can stand between us, except Mr Pantsful.

I am entirely curious to hear news of Mr Pea. My dear protégé, Nancy, has received a letter from Miss Fanny Sluttlike. She does indulge herself in writing to your Mr Pea, and I was about to rip that letter, when my eye caught a most favourable looking phrase. She said "No matter how hard I try to get into his pants, he still thinks of Isabella Pumpington and her many manual talents."

So you see my sweetest cousin, not all is lost; we are far superior to the society of Fanny and Nancy, for allowing them to be in our schemes. Why I for one, just last night, accidentally fed my lovely Nancy a laxative tea, so that she did not have to spend the evening with us, or be present at this morning's farewell. I am the last female presence in Reumaton that Mr Pantsful will remember.

One last thing: you will recall the beautiful marble bench that I mentioned afore; well that is now my beloved parents' shrine. What a remarkable idea that was, so that even now they can be useful to Reumaton Park.

With my deepest love,
Heather, etc.

Pumpington Park

My Darling Heather,

I write to you now with the greatest of news. Our esteemed uncle, Sir Phil Wuss, arrived in all manners, respectably in his horse and carriage. His presence here at Pumpington Park has had a remarkable effect on papa's disposition and, as I thought, he has decided to remain here for a couple of months to be in the company of papa for the summer.

As you may well remember, they have always been the fondest of companions, ever since first being introduced after the matrimony of my dearest parents. So many a summer has he spent here at Pumpington Park, what with him being alone and without a wife. It pains me to think of his last time here, when my dearly departed mother fell from the White Cliffs. I know that we have not spoken much of these matters, but I can tell you now, I remember well my mama leaving the house in a fluster that day. I saw her depart papa's dressing room, followed by Phil; I believe they had argued. It vexes me to think that she may have fallen due to not being in her best disposition.

But nay, let us talk of the future. Your Aragorn Pantsful sounds a charming young gentleman; you must write to him and insist on his joining us in Bath. As you may have heard from Nancy, Mr Pea means to stay there till I arrive, in order to join us in our group intercourses. I have received many a correspondence from him in the last week, and written in such a fine hand of a gentleman. He remarks on the personality of Fanny Sluttlike, and what a desperate creature she is. As always he fills his letters with prose as to my beauty and superiority in society. He sends his regards to you.

I have been spending many an hour taking turns in the garden now that spring is in full bloom. I met with the gardener and his son to discuss the plans for the memorial garden for mama. I declare that if it were not for his status, he being the son of a common gardener, Dickson would make me a fine companion during the summer evenings. He is way below what my status could possibly endure, but between the two of us, physically, I could endure him for many an hour.

Well my dear, I wait in anticipation for plans of our trip to Bath, as I know you will do well with your connections as to our accommodation. I can leave papa in the capable hands of Phil; I know that they will spend the summer evenings playing together, and many a day hunting in the vastness of Pumpington Park.

Reply hastily my dearest, and pray tell me news of Aragorn Pantsful.

Your dearest cousin,
Isabella

Bath

Dearest Isabella,

I succeeded in arriving in Bath yestereve, and my posture is already less aggravated.

Mr Pantsful has indeed returned to Reumaton Park last week, and he paid me a most gentle compliment, in singling me out, by offering me a place in his Barouche to Bath! He has some important business to attend to there, and insisted on me following him thither, in anticipation of your arrival. Since I have spoken at length of you during our intercourses in the shrubbery, he was most pleased to express his desire to be acquainted with you and Mr Pea.

Just on our last night in Reumaton, he volunteered to add a few drops of sleeping draught into dear Nancy's cup of tea, so that he could have the pleasure of a most amiable conversation with yours truly, without being hindered by her polite, though unnecessary, presence. The plan, however, turned very ill indeed, since dear Nancy actually drank from the wrong cup, resulting in Mr Pantsful employing the whole of the eve fast asleep on the silk couch, much to the disconcert of said Nancy, who could not explain to herself how such a gentleman could be so tired just by a turn in the shrubbery. I had to remind her hence of her low status and how the effects that any attempt to converse with a simpleton brain such as hers, would deplete the resources of many a gentlemen, even one as capable as Mr Pantsful. She immediately acknowledged the profound truth of my reasoning and resolved to improve her brain capacities by extensive embroidering. I was most pleased with her eagerness and, I might add, extremely diverted.

Since my arrival, Lady Felicity Ferocity has called on me every day, but I am anxiously awaiting your arrival, since your society is infinitely more agreeable then anybody else's.

Pray write soon to communicate your arrival.

Yours erectly,
Heather

Harrow Road, Bath

My Upstanding Cousin Heather,

My arrival here on Harrow Road has, as I imagined, caused immense excitement within the neighbourhood, which I am sure I have you to give thanks for, as I know that you have been passing news of my arrival around Bath. Already I have had the pleasure of a visit from Mr Pea, who was unfortunately in the company of Fanny Sluttlike and Nancy.

Well my darling, if it were not for your great mind, I would not have thought of popping a laxative into dear Fanny's tea, in order to get the company of Peawee to myself. I must say that as the colour drained from her face I did for a moment think her countenance actually improved, since her skin, unlike our own, is quite tanned, like that of a commoner. Peawee immediately offered his Barouche to take her home, and I quietly suggested to Nancy that it would have been unladylike of her to not have offered her assistance in such a moment, and accompany poor Fanny home.

The intercourses that followed that afternoon have indeed convinced me more than ever that Mr Pea means to make an offer of engagement this summer. How could I possibly refuse a gentleman of such high status in society, a gentleman so well read, a gentleman with just the right countenance to match my own. We do make a very fine couple indeed, and our presence in Bath, as well as yours and Mr Pantsful, will be the talk of summer society. I do so hope that our paths will cross tomorrow, but in case we shall not be alone, I must recollect to you my last few days at Pumpington Park, and the reasons for my hasty arrival in Bath.

I mentioned in my last letter my acquaintance with Dickson, the gardener's son. Well, I have received persistent attentions from him, and must say that despite finding him extremely attractive, I have found his remarks and, do not be shocked now, his physical advances, rather presumptuous considering his status in society. One evening, a few days before my departure, I had been riding my stallion, Darcy, in the company of Uncle Phil, when I returned to the stables to find Dickson waiting there, I can only assume to catch a glimpse of myself. He had the indecency to insist on helping me dismount Darcy, and in doing so touched my hand with his own. Well, my dear, I can assure you that our dear Uncle Phil had words with him on his conduct towards myself, and arranged immediately for my departure to Bath in a carriage, with a good friend of his, Sir William B Hard, who of course insisted on my calling him Willy.

He seems a sensible man of about seven or eight-and-thirty, and turns out he is an old and intimate friend of the family of your dear Mr Pantsful. On hearing of our acquaintance, and of you and Mr Pantsful being in Bath, he insists on us dining at his house this coming Saturday. I found him to be a fine, respectable gentleman and an alert companion on my journey here to Bath. He has a handsome estate in Scotland, along with a large inheritance and income which allow him to travel as he pleases. Since arriving in Bath he has been most attentive to me, and offered full use of his Barouche, and the presence of his company at any time I should be in need of it. His attentions flatter me, not that I wouldn't expect it from any gentleman, yet he makes my heart stop at the thought of not having his acquaintance for my own.

My dearest Heather, it is with this that I now fear that Mr Pea may be hasty in his procurement of an engagement with myself. You must help me find a way of hindering his attentions until I can steady my fluttering heart, and choose what title I shall take upon myself when I return to Pumpington Park at the end of the summer: Mrs Hard, or Mrs Pea?

Write hastily, and send word of your whereabouts tomorrow as I so wish to talk to you.

Your confused friend and cousin,

Isabella Pumpington

Bath

Dearest Isabella,

It gave me such pleasure, seeing you this afternoon in the Upper Rooms that I am now scarcely able to sleep. Therefore, I am taking this opportunity to write to you at present.

As you will recall, today we were not at liberty to converse about the information that you passed to me in your latest letter. Why, with dear Nancy, alongside Mrs and Miss Sluttlike imposing on us with such impoliteness, we could not find a moment for our private intercourse. Believe me, I did have words with Nancy upon our return to the apartment with regard to her inability to distract unwanted pursuers; however, I cannot be too severe with her, since I might have further use of her ingenuity.

I must confess I felt quite shocked upon hearing of the impertinence of young Mr Dickson! To dishonour his respectable, though low in status, father in such manner! Our dear uncle has acted most properly in dealing with the impudent rascal. I do believe that we are becoming too lenient with our servants. Why, we feed them and procure for them lodgings and what not; they should remember their place indeed!

Concerning your recent acquaintance with Mr Hard, believe me if I say that I was surprised! But do not fret; I am far from being displeased. Mr Pantsful has informed me that Mr Hard truly is a gentleman and very rich indeed! He has 30,000 a year! It is a most vexing situation having ones feelings so horizontally postured. One ought to know on whom to bestow one's graces, but this my dear, is a hard choice indeed! Mr Pantsful has readily agreed to accompany me to our Saturday party, and I dare say, I am very much anxious in anticipation.

However, I do believe that Miss Sluttlike, dear Nancy and Lord and Lady Ferocity will be at the party, since it would be considered very rude of Mr Hard if he were not to invite them. But do not fear, I might have a plan... By the by, did you notice the attire of Miss Sluttlike today? I cannot recall an uglier gown in my whole life! And those teeth! One should not be allowed in society with such misfortune.

As I was saying, Mr Pea left the Upper Rooms with dear Nancy and yours truly, hence I engaged him in conversation. I did perceive a most alarming willingness to secure your hand. I was pondering on how to refrain his plans for a time (so as to give you time to spend with Mr Hard) when a most unexpected thing happened! A very gentile lady, dressed in the latest fashion, stepped before us and gave a most surprised glance at Mr Pea! But that was nought compare with what happened to *his* complexion! His face flushed scarlet, while he fumbled a salutation in reply. He then regained his countenance, and introduced us to his acquaintance.

The lady in question, and very ladylike she was (though nought compared to you, dear cousin), is Miss Iona Hard, daughter of, hear this, Mr James Hard, of Hardington Park. She is the sister of your Mr Hard! How she became acquainted with Mr Pea I do not know, since he did not venture any explanation. But though their meeting was brief, Mr Pea left us in quite a state. I beg you, do discover all you can on the matter, since Miss Hard may well be in the position of procuring you the time you so feverishly seek. For once, we might discover some of the truth at the Saturday party, since her presence shall be most certain, given her connection.

I cannot attend the Rooms tomorrow since dear Nancy has required my presence on some personal business. She did not want to state the nature of said business, which aroused my curiosity greatly, but be sure I will keep you in the knowledge.

Write to me before we meet again, if you can.

With vexation, etc.
Heather

Harrow Road, Bath

My Benevolent Friend Heather,

It was indeed a delightful afternoon spent in the Upper rooms, despite being unable to take a turn in the gardens without the presence of the irritable Miss Sluttlike. I must have been somewhat out of sorts when I mentioned her as having a possible fairness to her countenance, as that afternoon her presence did nothing but vex me. I believe she should venture out into the summer air less, as the freckles on her face are becoming offensive to my eyes.

I do believe that Nancy has become a little too headstrong and should be more careful of whom she keeps company with. It was an astute move on your part to talk to her of this, I fear she may be led astray, and her business with you tomorrow yields perfect timing to converse with her further on the subject. If it is not beyond my station to say, I think she should spend more time comparing your countenance to Miss Sluttlikes, and then she must see what a grave choice she has made. I have no doubts that we could recommend to her a wiser choice of companion, although what she can possibly need more than what she receives from your dear self, I cannot imagine.

Your account of Mr Pea and the unaccountable nature of his relationship with Mr Hard's sister has vexed me greatly. That he has conversed throughout the winter with myself, and at the same time, without my knowing, with another, has done him no favours. Normally I would insist at once to have him tell me of the relationship; however, I must agree with you that, if I am astute, this situation will vindicate me in delaying his plans of a hasty engagement with myself.

After receiving your letter yestereve, my posture was acute, and knowing that I could hardly confront Mr Pea on the subject, I sent word to Mr Hard that I should like to take a turn with him in the park the following morning. He did converse with me on the subject of his sisters conduct of late; he seemed somewhat concerned for her, especially on the subject of a certain gentleman who he had heard had promised a public engagement with her this summer, but had since withdrawn it, causing her much grievance. He wishes that she spend some time in London over the forthcoming winter, in order to educate her. He believes her to be the unfortunate product of neglect due to the sad departure of both of their parents when she was but six years old. Mr Hard was unfortunately overwhelmed at that time by the procurement of the family estate and was ill advised by a close friend of the family to send her away to live with an Aunt until he was settled. This Aunt took advantage of the poor creature and did not educate her as she had promised to do. He has been afflicted with a bent posture for some time because of this, and holds himself solely responsible for her condition of late.

You, my dear, I am sure will understand his situation, as you yourself are in the position of responsibility of Nancy, therefore knowing of the hardship on one's own life at being left responsible for such an uneducated creature. I have never believed that the education of a young lady should ever befall a gentleman - his business on this earth lies elsewhere.

Mr Hard esteems himself more each time I have the pleasure of intercourse with him. He has an extremely favourable countenance, one with a story to tell. His account of his poor sister, and his concern for her, leaves me with a very disagreeable feeling towards Mr Pea, one that I am unsure of returning from. Every minute I spend with my darling Willy, every moment of intercourse, is a joy. When I am alone and without him, I find myself wondering of Willy B Hard, not of Mr Pea.

To end this discourse, I do believe that he is the gentleman of whom Mr Hard spoke, although he would mention no name. If there is any way for you to delve into the society of Nancy, as I know she is always conversing on the latest debaucheries to have happened in Bath, I would be forever grateful. I fear I cannot confront Mr Pea until I have a more definite conviction.

Your intrepid, yet vexed friend, with a posture bordering on the horizontal, yet upright when thinking of Mr Hard, endeavours you to reply hastily,

Isabella ...etc.

Harrow St, Bath

My dear Heather,

I have just this moment received a letter from Mr Hard which has skewed my posture beyond repair. The wretched Mr Pea has taken leave from Bath without a word to myself, the reason for which you can read in the following letter:

Stafford Street, Bath

My Dear Sweet Isabella,

It torments me that you must find me gone from Bath in a manner such as this. Forgive me for not having spoken to you in person, but a hasty departure had to be taken for the sake of my dear sister.

You will remember my telling you of the young gentleman to whom my sister was promised an engagement; I felt it out of my power to tell you his name that day, as I knew said gentleman to be a close acquaintance of yours. It grieves me to tell you that I have returned to my estate in Scotland in order to acquire the assistance of an old friend to take care of my sister during the period of her confinement! The gentleman responsible for her affliction, Mr Sean Pea, has vanished from his apartments in Bath. My plans do not go so far as to find his whereabouts, as I fear the repercussions of such an encounter. At present my sister's state of mind is the foremost thought in my own, with one exception: that is you, my dear Isabella. I am now afflicted with a posture, which on one part is bent to an extreme, and on the other has never been so erect. To find my dear sister so afflicted is a great injustice indeed; however, I can be at peace with the knowledge that you will now know the true nature of the barbaric Mr Pea.

That two such tender hearts as ours should now be separated vastly moves me. I implore you to write hastily as I yearn for your sweet discourse, but tease me not into temptation, for my duty must lie with Iona until I know her to be of a steady disposition once more. She is young and, despite her lacking the teachings of a fine lady like yourself, is a sturdy, headstrong girl; in my heart I must believe that she will prosper into a fine young lady, despite the treachery that has become her.

I am ever yours,

William B Hard

How a gentleman of Mr Pea's standing could do wrong to such exalted creatures as myself and Miss Iona Hard, I cannot conceive; unfortunately for Iona, she did!

And now, although finally having the decision of his conviction decided, I am convicted myself to being parted from a man who wishes to make love to me. I am beyond vexation and do believe that if I ever endeavour to lay my hands on the contemptible Mr Pea, he should be in fear of the repercussions, as I intend to purge the very part of him that has provoked this insupportable predicament.

Oh, to increase the severity of my disposition, I had cause just this moment to disrupt this letter due to a most unwanted visit from Fanny Sluttlike. Would you believe the contempt of her, she came with the false request of my company for a trip to London Street to purchase a new pelisse. I refused of course, stating that I had already ordered my new pelisses and was not in need of her company at this moment. She had the audacity to say to me "My dearest Isabella, I know of the business of Mr Pea and Miss Iona Hard and think it a contemptible affair indeed. I myself was inappropriately addressed by him on more than one occasion, but knowing him to be below my standards for a companion, disregarded his innumerable proposals. I only wish that I had given more warning to you, my dearest friend".

Well, this statement astounded me. As we both know, she was given to throwing herself into his arms on numerous occasions, but being the lady that I am, I composed myself and invited her in for tea, only to give her a triple dose of laxative and then send her out into the street without carriage, saying that I had forgotten a prior engagement this afternoon. I refuse to have Fanny Sluttlike converse with me as if I were her inferior, and to say that I am in need of her advice. Oh, am I so terrible my dearest Heather? Do tell me that I was not impudent but, rather, justifiable in my actions.

Your affectionate friend entreats you always in your delicate refinement and requests consoling in her time of vexation,

Isabella

Bath

Isabella, Isabella, oh Isabella,

What evil has befallen our family? Upon receiving your latest, I was truly not myself for a time. Dear useless Nancy could not comprehend my sudden change in posture and was at loss as to what to do. She thusly decided to take up embroidery, so that her inferior brain might receive illumination. However, that did not procure any better knowledge for her. Finally it dawned on her to fetch me a cup of tea and my smelly salts...dear oh dear... Her mind is evolving at the same rate as that of a platypus in its embryonic stage.

Showing a countenance, a posture, a brightness proper of a lady, I directly sent her to fetch dear Pantsful. He hastened to me with the speed of an eagle in the mating season, and holding my gloved hand, enquired after my vexed posture.
Pray cousin, forgive me, but I had to show him Mr Hard's letter concerning his amiable sister and the treacherous Mr Pea.

Upon finishing the letter, he resolved to leave at once for Scotland, so as to offer his service to his

Hard friend. He was pained to take leave of my company, but he deemed it necessary to resolve the unfortunate affair speedily, and hence return his friend to your society. What noble heart beats under that camel skin of his, what awesome equipment pulses in that name of his… I was moved to tears indeed!

Mr Pantsful ordered Nancy to care for me to the best of her brain's capacity. What is more (and this advice was indeed curious), he suggested that neither of us ladies should speak again with Miss Fanny Sluttlike! Upon my word! He would not say more on the subject, but I caught him bestowing a sharp glance to Nancy before he ran through the door (literally).

Immediately after his departure, which left my heart empty and my front door scarred for life, I cornered Nancy and insisted upon knowing the truth behind that glance. Ladylike as I am, I threatened her with the wearing of leaden bloomers until her eight-and-tenth birthday if she did not speak the truth. And believe me, they do not go at all well with a lace gown.

Now, dear Isabella, do please sit down, for what I am about to tell you may vex your hairstyle beyond repair. As you recall, Nancy wanted my confidence for matters of a personal nature. It turns out that our vulgar common acquaintance Fanny Sluttlike is with child! Mr Pea's child! There. I said it. However, it is far more complicated than it seems. Fanny learned of Mr Pea's heart being taken firstly with Iona Hard, then with you. She could not stand the rejection and plotted a scheme so unspeakable, that even I could not have planned it. Even Nancy was shocked, so much so that her corset exploded!

Fanny had resolved to invite Mr Pea to her apartment in Bath, a month ago, and had him drink a sleeping draught concealed in his tea. When the gentleman collapsed on the carpet, she took advantage of him in a sailor's fashion! Hence the child was so dementedly conceived! I do not know how he came to perform. I am truly puzzled. However, the situation is thus: Mr Pea ignores his fatherhood, and has left Bath simply on the account of the situation with your good self and Iona Hard. He is reflecting upon his future course of action. Miss Sluttlike will have to conceal her motherhood, since she is presently (and possibly eternally, if you ask me) a maiden. And our gentlemen, our source of joy and intercourse in the shrubberies, have gone…

Pray, advise me on how to deal with the impertinence of Miss Sluttlike, since I do not believe laxative to be of rightful use at the present, considering what she is carrying!

Your lonely cousin, with a posture rotating at ten yards per second,
Heather.

Harrow St, Bath

My Dearest Heather,

How can I possibly convey my vexation at such a calamity? I have not allowed myself to leave my apartments here on Harrow Street for at least a week now. To think that the dreaded Miss Sluttlike had the impertinence to show face to me after what she had done, knowing that I should hear of it imminently through the thread of society, such that I weave. It is now no surprise to me that she is in need of a new pelisse or two, sewn together no doubt, so that it shall fit her in her stolen state of confinement.

No more than an hour after your letter reached me, I heard from an acquaintance that a doctor had been fetched late in the night to the Sluttlike residence. Mrs Sluttlike had taken to a fit of fainting after learning of her daughters' predicament, and had to be sedated. What a wretched state of affairs, to have all four of your daughters in such a quandary, and all at the same time. At least she has peace of mind that the younger Sluttlikes must have at the least plundered their confinement from their husbands. As Mrs Sluttlike's eldest daughter, Fanny has disgraced her family name beyond repair. They say that one should blossom in countenance at this time; well, if this be true then it shall be Fanny's one and only chance of pleasing the gentlemen's eyes I am sure, but think what a poor countenance her illegitimate child will have. One can only pray that it will have a little of Mr Pea, although then it will still have the poorest of dispositions. I can no longer bear to contemplate the matter further.

I have received word from Willy B Hard, from his estate in Scotland. Your devoted Mr Pantsful arrived there one week after so hastily departing through your door; by the by, I do hope that you have managed to replace said door as you never know what degenerates walk the streets at night. Our gentlemen wish us to take leave of Bath imminently and join them at Hardington Park for the rest of the summer season. I hear that Hardington Park has been, and still is, extremely popular with high society over the years, even after the departure of Sir Hard, and I believe that this will be a great opportunity for us to rid our minds of the likes of Fanny Sluttlike. Willy endeavours to have us both, and of course dear Nancy, as this will be a good opportunity for her to join the intercourses of high society. Despite all those that will be there, I hear that Hardington Park has many a shrubbery for intimate intercourse.

A close acquaintance of your Mr Pantsful, Reverend Knight, will be travelling up to Hardington to take a living there, and he leaves Bath at the end of the week. He has room for all three of us, and more importantly, I had the idea that Nancy should be a perfect companion for him when we arrive in Hardington.

I wait with anticipation for your reply,

Your friend Isabella

Hardington Park

Dear Isabella,

I am slowly recovering from the vexation of the past afternoon, when our merry party was so unkindly dispersed by the uncouth behaviour of our barouche driver. The simpleton not only killed the poor horse, and very nearly all of us along with it, but he was also incapable of procuring us another barouche! A mere two small peasant carts he was able to find for us ladies (the ineptitude!), thereby depriving me and Nancy of your joyous company, and thus leaving the poor Reverend Knight at the side of the road to bury the horse and wait for a third cart!

'Mr Hard will hear about this!' I was thusly thinking with rising frustration, when I beheld the sight of Hardington Park! What an ailment it was for my oblique posture. And to think that one day you could be mistress of all that!

'See Nancy,' I told my protégé. 'This is the sort of dwelling where respectable people breed. You should consider yourself fortunate. In fact, before retiring to your bed tonight, I command you to stand before the looking glass and repeat ten times: "I am a fortunate girl, and do not deserve such kindness." Nancy, of course, was so excited at the thought of improving herself she even ventured to propose that she will do it every night of our staying at Hardington, and will ask both myself and yourself, for new sentences to repeat each night.

Upon arriving at the entrance of the house, your darling Mr Hard welcomed us warmly, no doubt on your account. He is a rare gentleman and felt so mortified at our misfortune on the road that he decided to flagellate the barouche driver as the after-dinner entertainment. However, I believe you should make him change his mind, dear cousin, before we sit down for dinner. As it is, Mr Pantsful was regarding me with his oceanic eyes, and I truly had to contain myself, since the mere sight of him sent flutters down my petticoat.

Mr Hard informed us that you had preceded us and were presently freshening yourself for dinner, since we were to have the honour of making the acquaintance of several illustrious guests who were to be staying at the house for a few weeks. I might have said that the honour would be theirs in meeting us, dear cousin! I enquired after Miss Iona Hard and was happy to learn that, although she prefers to keep herself in her quarters, she is recovering slowly but steadily.

Mr Pantsful presently ushered me into the house, and I noticed a new curious locket around his manly neck. Upon my enquiry he replied: "Dear Lady Mouthful, the jewel contains a shard of your wooden door from Bath. I found it embedded in my skull upon my arrival in Scotland, and could not part with it… literally. It reminded me of our last meeting too much." What countenance and pride he displayed upon conversing with me.

As soon as I took possession of my quarters, I decided to quickly write you. I believe that, except for few blessed moments, we shall never be alone and at freedom to discuss our business. What with Nancy, our gentlemen, and all the guests … Therefore cousin, pray write to me! I want to discover who the guests are! And by the by, I do hope Reverend Knight will join us for dinner. He has been a most pleasant companion on the road today, and I believe your suggestion of Nancy as his companion during our stay at Hardington is a viable solution. At least it will keep us free to entertain ourselves in the shrubberies with all the guests.

I wonder what to wear this evening …

Soon, my dear Isabella.

Hardington Park

Dearest impeccable Isabella,

What an ordeal I had! But let me recount to you the events of this wretched past night.

The evening started quiet remarkably. What an exquisite dinner we enjoyed. Your Mr B. Hard truly is the perfect host! Those wood pigeons were delicious and although rather famished-looking, they were marvellously presented, what with those tiny silky petticoats and velvety coats! Indeed all the guests seemed to enjoy themselves in undressing them! That is, all except Reverend Knight. The poor man was rather embarrassed at the prospect of publicly removing a petticoat, even if the lady in question was of the flying variety! And did you notice how Nancy was observing the gentleman, as if she wanted to aid him, but without the courage to address him at the table?! I therefore whispered to her to not be shy and show him. And what do you think she did? She tapped him lightly on the shoulder and then proceeded to lift her own petticoat! I wish you could have seen the Reverend's face - he turned all beetrooty and I truly thought he would pass on at the dining table!

I had to restrain a hearty laugh and threw an icicle glance at my witless protégé. You should have seen how she kept quietly to a corner for the rest of the evening, staring at the embroidery on one of the armchairs, and taking notes. Sometimes I wonder how she would manage to live if I wasn't there to remind her to inhale … However, and here I must beg your full attention, at the time of retiring to our quarters, something rather curious happened.

I was walking Nancy to her chambers, reminding her of the smallness of her brain in comparison to those wood pigeons. We stood outside her door for some time, while I gave her the phrase she was to repeat ten times that night. In light of the recent events I set it thusly: "I am never to show my petticoat to a Reverend, unless a marriage proposal has been forwarded and accepted by the superior brain of my mentor."

Once Nancy had retired, I went to my own chambers, and as I was closing the door, a remarkable thing happened! In the dimness of the corridor a tall figure, clad in white, glided past my door and disappeared at the end of the corridor, where the painting of Mr Willy B. Hard's dad hunting naked in the shrubberies hangs. In fact, unless I was very much deceived by the alcohol of the night, the apparition disappeared *through* the painting!

Only my strict, superior lady's self-discipline allowed me not to scream and, upon locking the door of my room, I sought refuge under the bed, where I fell asleep after some time (please keep this particular to your understanding self, as I feel ashamed at that memory).

So, my dear, it is early morning now, and I know this letter will be delivered to you with your breakfast. I strongly desire your company as soon as is convenient, as I am still badly shaken. Pray, do not disclose this event to anybody, not even our host, as I want to discuss the matter with you first.

Shakily yours,
Heather

Hardington Park

My dearest Heather,

I have been endeavouring to reply to your letter of this morning ever since the conclusion of our morning meal. Were it not for Sir Ramsbottom's usual unwanted attentions to myself, I should have at the least been able to spend a little time in discourse with you; alas we were forced from company due to the bumbling fool once more most uncouthly arising amid our fellow guests to attend me to a place at his side, and with Lady Ramsbottom so close to the end of her confinement! By the by, she was indeed two times the paleness of your dear self. I am sure that had my Willy been there he should have dealt with the matter swiftly, and firmly.

I must also note the absence of the Reverend and Nancy this morning; I do believe I heard word of them having departed for an early morning turn in the shrubberies. I must say that, despite my agreeable nature as to the good properties of the morning air, I am unsure that it be wholly appropriate for her to be taking intercourses in the shrubberies alone with even a gentleman of the Reverend's standing. I think, with your approval as a matter of course, it would be wise as such for her to partake in a few lines in front of the looking glass, perhaps something along the lines of: "Intercourse between an upstanding young lady as myself and the Reverend should only be taken when my mentor is there to guide me."

Now, my dear, to the matter at hand - it has been the strangest of days and I fear that, as yet, your Pantsful and my Hard have not yet returned from their business in town. It is late and I am in my room in the Western Wing, where my little writing desk looks over the flower gardens, and again, it is raining and the fog is as thick as that of Nancy's mind.

You must recall how, on our first evening here, we were so unsure of the atmosphere that had met us in the Northern Wing during our explorations; I recall our relief on hearing that we were to stay in a separate side of the manor, in the Western Wing. As you know, it is a great distance; so much so that it takes Mr B Hard's Grandmother the best part of the day just to get herself from one side to the other. How she does dote on the painting of her husband that you mentioned.

Since our arrival, I have had little want to venture again into the midst of the Northern Wing but, after your experiences of the last night, I do believe it warrants our attention for, if the apparition was in fact that of the late Sir Hard Senior, he quite possibly has need of communicating with his dear wife; I shouldn't be surprised, if he in his departed state were as frail as his wife be now in life, then they may have been chasing one another since the day he died without ever catching up. And, my dear Heather, if the apparition were not he, then pray, who might it have been, and what need do they have for still being here, trapped so, between the living and whatever lies beyond our present state of being.

I pray that your state of perplexity be improved when we next meet, I believe we must endeavour to perform some manner of séance so that we might attempt to communicate with this unearthly being and settle our minds as to what it seeks in

Hardington Manor. I am unsure as to how a suggestion of this sort would be met by our fellow guests here, but I am sure that we will be in need of a few associates if we are to partake in said séance.

Yours,

Isabella

Hardington Park, My room

Dearest cousin,

What incredible events have befallen us in the past night! I am still so truly vexed that you have been taken ill since yestereve, but very much relieved that you are now back with yours truly. Upon receiving your letter in the afternoon, I resolved to visit you in your chambers but, as I approached the Western wing, a servant told me of your sudden indisposition. The servant knew not what had befallen you, except that Sir Ramsbottom had carried you from the shrubberies back to the house claiming that you had suddenly lost consciousness. Immediately after placing your dear body onto the bed, he took a carriage and left for town on account of business of the most urgent manner, thus leaving all women unattended at Hardington Manor.

What lack of breed! Of course, there is always the Reverend, but he does have duties towards the congregation, and therefore he cannot always be in our company. I sent a maid to fetch Nancy at once, and sat at your bedside with trepidation and fear for your health. How I suffered to see you so still and unresponsive, and how useless I felt! What, with my bent posture I couldn't even sit properly.

Nancy came as quick as she could after two hours. Her sense of orientation is as unfortunate as her bee-sized brain, and what do you think? She got lost, of course! However, Lady Iona Hard found her in the East Wings almost in tears, and very kindly put aside her own concerns for her confinement to return her to me. As they were entering, Lady Ramsbottom happened upon them and so it was that the other three ladies of the house were all gathered in your room to wait on you (Lady Iona's mother was in her chamber, not to be disturbed). I could not give them any news of your state, as I was in the dark about the circumstances of how you were taken ill, but Lady Iona resolved at once to send for the doctor. What presence of mind is harboured in that lovely fragile creature, indeed if she was to be your future sister in-law, I would not have any objections whatsoever.

Lady Ramsbottom and myself went with her on this errand and I left Nancy to sit by your side. Unfortunately, that dreaded fog that you saw from your parlour was now surrounding the Manor, preventing the doctor or, for that matter, our dearest gentlemen to come to us. Again Lady Iona showed her readiness of mind by ordering that a light dinner be brought to us all in your parlour, so that you should not be left unattended. Upon returning to your chambers a dreadful spectacle left us rooted inside the doorway! You were lying atop the bedcovers, with your arms folded across your chest, composed as one would a dead body. Many candles were surrounding your bed and Nancy ... Nancy ... was kneeling next you in prayer. I can scarcely believe I survived that moment, as you looked to our eyes as though you were dead. Then suddenly you took a breath, which scared us even more! And yet, at that moment the reality of what I was witnessing hit me: that incompetent, ignorant, brainless protégé of mine, had thought you *were* dead, and had proceeded to prepare your corpse accordingly! With an elegant and ladylike movement I jumped at her throat and began the strangling process, a horizontal, rapid shaking of her head through the positioning of my hands upon her too-long neck. Only the presence of the ladies saved her from serious death. I thereafter recomposed myself, smelled my salts, adjusted my hair and sat in the armchair. Nancy kneeled at my feet begging for me to terminate her simpleton existence since, and these are her own words, "No matter how much I try, I will never be a lady. I will never be as perfect as you, Lady Heather, or as Lady Isabella. My brain is just not big enough. Please allow me to take my life." As you know, I would never let anything happen to her, at least not until I am through with her. As you know, I took a vow to turn her into a lady and until I accomplish said titanic feat, I will not rest. As punishment, I ordered her to wear the dreaded lead bloomers for a week, together with the lead shoes I ordered for her for situations such as this, four-and-twenty hours a day. Very obligingly she went to put them on at once. Moreover, she was to repeat in front of the looking glass ten times per night the following sentence: "I will not declare someone deceased before a doctor or the superior brain of my master has said so."

After this turmoil had passed, we took a little refreshment in your presence, and with the help of a good dose of strong fortified wine all around, I made the two ladies aware of the strange apparition of the night before. Lady Ramsbottom was in such a flutter that she took a swig of wine from the bottle and didn't let go of it until she passed out flat on the floor. What breed …

However, that left yours truly at liberty to discuss the matter further with Lady Iona. I could easily tell that this was not the first time she was hearing of such episode either. Indeed she confirmed, albeit reluctantly, that a similar incident had happened to her but one day before our arrival. Discussing such matters with you still lying there, like a corpse, was rather unsettling, so we put a cover over you, so as not to be distressed too much. It was now past the midnight, and we decided that a séance should be arranged for the following evening, since it was important to have you in the party.

It is now past lunch, and you are recovered again. None of the gentlemen will return until tomorrow. Tonight, after our supper, your good self, yours truly, Lady Ramsbottom, Lady Iona and Nancy will attempt to contact the late Sir Hard in front of his portrait. Lady Iona believes that one of her servants, a cook, is known in the village for her skills as a medium, so she will be our guide during the séance. The fog is still thick around the manor, and that does not bode well. An ominous sign indeed. Moreover, Nancy's new leaded outfit is creating such noises in the house, with every step she takes, that it sounds like the manor is being trampled by a herd of oxen! Why, even the Reverend heard the echoing boom of her shoes from his parsonage and came running to ascertain that the manor was still standing.

We did not disclose our plans to him, as we have yet to decide if a man's presence is needed or not. I am concerned about the condition of Lady Iona: in her delicate state she should not attempt such endeavours, but she is resolute, and besides, it was her father after all. I only hope this cook woman does wash. I could not stand an evening in the company of an inferior breed who smells badly.

I shall wait for you at the dinner table, and pray. If you can, you must tell me what happened to you in the shrubberies yester-morning. I am extremely puzzled and, of course, vexed beyond belief.

Yours, Heather.

Hardington Park

Heather,

I had little chance at dinner to inform you thoroughly of my near demise in the shrubberies, as I had not want of our company being fearful more than they need be. Therefore, I have tried to account for all the events below, I do feel strongly that as these events unfold it would make good sense to keep a written record, as it may well be of use as we attempt to unthread the history of Hardington Manor ...

That afternoon, I retired to my chamber as I had been feeling of a restless nature and, so venturing to my writing desk with the idea to compose a letter of sweet nothings to my dear Willy, I looked out into the gardens, and beyond to the shrubberies, where the fog lay thick. As I sat there composing my letter, my posture was slighted by what I thought I saw entering the shrubberies: Nancy.

The fog had seemed to sink to the ground, forming a thick layer through which I caught a glimpse of her white bonnet. Well, to my dismay I had found myself in the position of feeling responsible for her, and being her superior, and not of want to disturb you, I intrepidly left my chamber for the gardens alone, in order that I may fetch the wretched girl before she made a spectacle of herself ... again! Well, my darling, had I the fortune of premonitions I would have been in the mind to leave the witless girl to the peril that she deserves, and almost must compare myself to her in my stupidity at following her alone into the fog. As I entered the shrubberies I glimpsed back towards the manor to see a light go on in the North wing. Curious as it was, I was only able to resolve one mystery at a time so I decided to enter the shrubberies, fetch Nancy, give her the hiding of her feeble and, what will be, miserable life if I have anything to do with it, and return her to the manor to put out the dreaded light in the North Wing.

Hence, back to the shrubberies my mind did go. It felt as though I had been wandering for some time when I heard the faint sound of intercourse ahead of me, and as I turned the corner I heard Nancy;

she seemed to be talking with someone, yet they must have been of an extremely stunted nature as they could not be seen above the fog, and before I could form some abuse of the verbal kind, never mind physical, she appeared and she turned to me. She was looking in horror at me, then she was gone, pulled down into the fog, and all had turned quiet.

It must have been a mere moment later that I felt a hand on my shoulder. My posture was frozen in the instant I beheld the creature that had touched me. Firstly, my thoughts were that she was Nancy, yet she looked like the fog itself, as if she was the fog, or was enveloped within the fog, and her touch was cold, as much so as the look one would get from Fanny if one ever slighted her. Instead, stood before me was a peasant girl, the offence of her having touched me made worse by her countenance, which was of a kind that I had never the misfortune of coming upon before then. Her eyes were sunken and black, and she wore the same bonnet as Nancy, though hers was in need of some serious laundering. I am glad to say that she had little time for attempted converse with me before my head was well ahead of the rest of my body, on its way down to the ground where I must have lain till Sir Ramsbottom found me.

To think that I had lain there, unconscious, and in the presence of an unbred woman, who was also possibly, by all accounts ... dead!!! I know not what became of Nancy, for, as you told me, she was found in the North wing … in tears; what I do know, is what will become of her, and preferably before we embark on our séance, since then she may be of some use to us from the "other" side. I would like to hear the reasoning behind her removal from the shrubberies, whilst I lay cold on the ground!!!! If she thinks that her lead bloomers are a weight to carry, she had better have a good explanation as to her behaviour, as my posture was horizontal when I awoke, and to hear that it had been Sir Ramsbottom whom had happened upon me in the shrubberies.

One thought I have had, but have pushed to the back of my mind, is Lord Ramsbottom's stature! I need not go into a full explanation of that - if Nancy is cavorting with a Lord, a married one at that **...** it would explain his presence in the shrubberies.

 I suggest that we interrogate Nancy, and then go ahead with the séance as planned, tonight. This must be concluded before the gentlemen return for I fear that they would think us mad if they heard of our plans to contact the dead! Although, I think Willy would rather I speak to the dead, than the inbred!!!

Until tonight then, my dear Heather, and dress well, for if this is to be our last night, let us at least cross over adorned, as we deserve. If I had to live out eternity in a dirty white bonnet I should at least have the courtesy to haunt those of my own kind … the disrespect!

Yours, violated,

Isabella

Hardington Park

My sweet cousin,

I can scarcely be still after the exciting events of this past night. Indeed, not even the scandalous society of Bath could have given us such flutters of the petticoats! I trust by now you have regained your usual perfect composure and appearance, as we will soon have the pleasure of dining with our fine gentlemen. At your request, I have endeavoured to keep a written account of these past events, so as to put our thoughts in order, before we provide said gentlemen with an account of our deeds since their departure from the manor. I am now asking you to read the part concerning the events of last night, so as to confirm that I have not forgotten any detail, or been deceived by said strange occurrences.

After our dinner, I took dear Nancy to my chambers, and with the threat of cutting off all of her hair and forging with them a pair of sideburns for her face, in retaliation for her abandoning you, I ordered her to recount her mysterious escapade into the shrubberies. As you had suspected, she had indeed been lured there by Sir Ramsbottom, with the pretence of observing a rare bird that only appears where the fog is really thick. On this note I took the opportunity to remind her that in that event she could have just closed her eyes and imagined her brain, for where else is such fog to be found? She nodded at the veracity of the statement for a few minutes. Eventually she reported of the same strange vision you had, that of a dirty, bonneted head, spying on them from a nearby bush. The apparition then seemed to walk towards her, and in horror she ran away. At first I believed that the moving form had been none other than you, approaching her, but since your bonnet would always be immaculately clean, I then deduced that the first vision had been that of the dead girl you saw soon after, prior to your fainting.

At that moment Lady Iona called upon us, for she wanted us to meet with her cook, who had been informed of our intentions. As you were caring for Lady Ramsbottom, who was still recovering from the three bottles of fortified wine she had drunk to steady her nerves, I attended the meeting. While Nancy was trying to lubricate her lead bloomers, so as to acquire a certain composure in her walk, the cook told us that we should gather around the portrait of the naked Sir Hardy as soon as was convenient. Although I cannot abide an inferior telling me how to act, I sent Nancy to call upon your good self and, indeed on this note, there have been many instances during this long night in which both of us have performed a level of manual labour that is really not proper for ladies of our magnitude, but it was all endured for the greatness of the cause.

So it was that the ladies, and a cook, of Hardington Manor, gathered around the portrait with trepidation and unease. As you recall, Nancy was wearing a lead bonnet for the occasion, therefore I presently placed four candles on her head, so as to make her feel useful, and to show her my affection. We then held hands and let the cook perform her duties. At the moment in which the ghost of Sir Hardy appeared however, Lady Ramsbottom fainted theatrically, displacing Nancy's already precarious equilibrium, and they both fell to the ground, extinguishing the candles, and leaving us all in the dark. The light emanating from the ghost was strong enough for us to observe him whispering to the cook, who nodded her understanding of the situation. He then disappeared and Lady Iona, although very shocked at the sight of her dear departed father, asked us to follow her into her chambers, an action that took longer than it should have, since we had to drag the heavy Lady Ramsbottom across the floor.

In the chambers, the cook revealed the horrible truth to us. At the time of the birth of Mr Will B. Hard, the late Sir Hardy took an unseemly fancy for his son's young wet nurse, probably induced by the recurrent sight of her breasts-aplenty. On a foggy day, Sir Hardy was taking a turn in the shrubberies, when he came upon the unaccompanied wet nurse. What was left of his masculine impulse took over his mind and, without ceremony, he used her very ill indeed, in sailor's fashion, right there and then! However, his wife, Lady Hard, had also decided to take a turn in her grounds and, filled with horror, stumbled upon her naked husband and the girl. She returned to the manor in haste, and for three days she locked herself in her chambers to paint her brutal husband! She then hung the painting just outside his chamber, so as to give him a hint of her being in the knowledge of his action.

Sir Hard was forced to resolve the matter at once, before the scandal could leave the venerable walls of Hardington Manor. He therefore lured the wet nurse into that same spot in the shrubberies, with the promise of an elopement! The poor, silly, ignorant, dirty girl, thinking that her life was about to change for the better, consented to the secret meeting. Alas, her miserable life was indeed about to change, but not as she had expected. With blind fury, Sir Hard kissed her and in doing so he placed his hands on her greasy neck and took her life from her! He then buried her behind a bush and walked back to the manor. As he walked in haste, he saw a light being put out in the North wing, a sign that his wife knew she had been vindicated. I do believe Isabella, that it was the same light you saw as you were walking along the grounds two mornings before.

As the cook finished with her tale, Lady Iona became understandably pale, but you have to agree that her resolute spirit was very strong indeed, for allowing her to follow through with our plans. We agreed that a proper burial should be granted to the miserable girl. As Nancy was sent to retrieve the infamous painting of Sir Hard, the cook went to fetch two shovels and lights. When we were all gathered at the main door, we resolved to take a turn to the dreaded bush. As all those who had

71

partaken in the séance needed to be present, we required Lady Ramsbottom's presence still. As she was still fainted, we dumped her body into the gardener's wheel barrel and took her with us (I am expecting great rewards from the hag for all the strength that we wasted on her).

On reaching the bush, the unexpected appearance of Reverend Knight sent us all into a frenzy! Why, we thought that he was the ghost of Sir Hard, coming to stop us! Hence, we all attacked the poor man! Petticoats were flying here and hair was flying there, and Nancy even hit him with the shovel! Eventually, the Reverend managed to free himself, and when we came to our senses, we actually realised that a man of the cloth was essential to performing a proper burial. Glad that we had not killed him, Lady Iona ordered him to prepare for a funeral. His staring eyes gave no indication of whether he thought the funeral was for himself, or indeed for Lady Ramsbottom, who was still in the wheel barrel, showing off her intimate laces. As Lady Iona endeavoured to explain the situation, dear Nancy was kindly asked to help the cook in un-burying the girl's body.

Dawn was fast approaching when the skeleton of the wet nurse came into sight. We placed the painting over it and, as the Reverend performed his clergyman's duty, Lady Iona asked Nancy to set fire to both. Since Nancy's brain had already worked well beyond its natural capacity, I realised just in time that I needed to clarify the situation for her benefit. 'Dear Nancy,' I said. 'Before I decide to use your nostril hairs as kindling, please reflect upon the request of Lady Iona. When she said "both" she meant the skeleton and the painting … not yourself and the Reverend …' Nancy, visibly relieved, stopped pouring oil over her own gown and instead poured it into the pit. The cook threw a lit candle into it and, as the flames of purification leapt toward the sky, a piercing scream came from the house! We hastily returned to the manor, where a servant informed us that the corpse of Lady Hard had been found in the North wing. It was at that moment that Mr Pantsful and Mr B. Hard arrived upon us. What a spectacle we must have been: a cook, a reverend, five ladies, one of whom was in a wheel barrel, out of bed so early, covered in dirt and smelling of smoke, all at loss for words. Luckily the gentlemen allowed us to retire, postponing the explanation for later.

I shall go and pay my regards to my camel-skinned man. How I have missed his far-gazing eyes and manly scent … Why, I believe myself to be in love! Oh, if only we can have our dreams realised, and both be engaged before the end of this stay.

Your, for once unvexed cousin,

Heather

Harrow Road, Bath.

Illustrious Mr Hard and Mr Pantsful,

 I must begin by apologising to you for having the impudence of writing to your excellent selves. Your eyes must be watering at the sight of my surely improper and vile calligraphy. Alas, my most beloved Lady Heather and her superb dearest of friends, Lady Isabella, have ordered me to do so, under threat of a month wearing my leaden bloomers. Once again, forgive me.

Lady Heather and Lady Isabella have asked that I bestow upon you their gratitude at allowing them to wholly arrange and execute the wedding plans. Undoubtedly, as the ladies of society that they are, they knew that the family Hard, and Pantsful ladies, would have been much vexed had the day's affairs not been up to their feminine expectations. Any lady knows, no matter where her current posture in society lies, that these matters do not bode well if left to the male society.

Lady Heather explained to me, as she often is required to do a number of times before I am able to understand, that the day would not have contained all those delicate intricacies that a lady's touch so undoubtedly gives, had its planning been given over unto a gentleman's hands. They both told me, whilst blushing a most splendid colour of English Rose pink, that you both were knowingly aware of their ladylike touch. Hence, the guest list having consisted of Bath's most prominent and, what can only be described as the highest of English society, it was indeed a gracious affair because of this, and the intercourses on the day were also indeed sumptuous.

I must therefore convey the apologies of both Lady Heather and Lady Isabella for having left the altar in such haste, on the day of the wedding. You see, they had had word from a close acquaintance that a certain property had become available in Bath, and they were eager to secure the deal. They were however sure that you would both understand and that you would not find it vexing to spend your honeymoons in the company of one another.

My Masters, as I shall refer to the aforementioned ladies from here onward, have finally opened their business, to the amazement of the society of Bath. As you recall, the séance performed on the grounds of Hardington Park was a large success, to the point that Mr Hard senior's soul was actually put to rest properly and in accordance with civilised rules. This success has thusly worked its way into the fertile minds of my superiorly endowed Masters, exhorting them to pursue this enterprise on a larger scale. It is therefore with joy, trepidation and goodwill that I am proud - although unworthy - to announce to your Graces that "The Ladylike Way to Eternity" has officially opened for business!

The best of Bath society attended the grand opening and I am sure that the event will be talked of forever after. The property has a fine prospect in the cemetery - as is proper for a business such as this - and it is most graciously decorated. Truly, my Masters have not worried about expenses ... which reminds me Mr Hard, you might want to consider selling a few of your Scottish properties ...

We had a sumptuous buffet for our guests, which was a resounding success. I have no doubt it is down to the personal touch and superior breeding of my Masters. Speaking of personal touch, it was they who showed their superiority by personally reserving a special dish of Laxo-cupcakes for the entire Sluttlike family. How marvellous. I truly wish I grow to be even a little like them, as it would bring some consolation to my poor mother who has been crying since the day of my birth, when she first gazed upon me, although I could never explain why.

The Masters bid me to tell you they shall be with you both at Hardington Park upon your return from your honeymoons, where they will be anxious to hear all about your many intercourses in the Lake District. I was also told to apologise at least ten times about my writing to you, but since the Masters were far too busy embalming a corpse - (one of the many services offered by their business) so that at least in death one may have the appearance of a lady (or a gentleman) - it could not have been helped.

Farewell your Graces,

And may the Ladylike glow shine upon your heads always.

Your devoted, although bungling, ham-fisted, inept, useless, futile, worthless, insignificant, wretched and miserable Nancy - lying at your feet, carpet style, and you don't even have to stand still.

ABOUT THE AUTHOR

Visit the author's official website:

www.ftbarbini.com

81

82

Lightning Source UK Ltd.
Milton Keynes UK
UKOW07f1839150215

246308UK00005B/37/P